Lucy's Secret

For my mother

Groundwood Books / Douglas & McIntyre
720 Bathurst Street, Suite 500, Toronto, Ontario M5S 2R4
Distributed in the USA by Publishers Group West
1700 Fourth Street, Berkeley, CA 94710

We acknowledge for their financial support of our publishing program the Canada Council for the Arts, the Government of Canada through the Book Publishing Industry Development Program (BPIDP), the Ontario Arts Council and the Government of Ontario through the Ontario Media Development Corporation's Ontario Book Initiative.

The author wishes to thank the Conseil des arts et des lettres du Québec for financial support.

National Library of Canada Cataloging in Publication
Levert, Mireille
Lucy's secret / Mireille Levert.
ISBN 0-88899-566-0
I. Title.
PS8573.E956355L83 2004 jC813'.54 C2003-903468-2

Design by Michael Solomon
Printed and bound in China

The illustrations are in watercolor and gouache acrylic on Lanaquarelle paper.

Lucy's Secret

Mireille Levert

A Groundwood Book

Douglas & McIntyre • Toronto Vancouver Berkeley

The gate is open.

Anna Zinnia's smile calls, "Come in."

I see bugs flitting and flying, sipping nectar from flowers and crawling through the garden.

Ferocious wild beasts lie in wait. I make my way past them.

Anna Zinnia calls softly, "Look, Lucy. Let's see what we can find in the tree of life. I'll show you a secret."

When I open the box, I see little shining seeds.

"In each seed lies a hidden baby flower," says Anna Zinnia.

"How can it be born?" I ask.

"Make a little hole in the soil. Put the seed in. Cover it with earth and water it gently. There you are. But the secret lies in the waiting," insists Anna Zinnia.

"The baby plant is sleeping inside its seed. Sometimes it needs some sun. Sometimes it needs some rain. Watch and listen to nature," says Anna.

"The earth is dry," I say, listening. "Let's dance for rain. Almost a whole day has gone by. Are they born yet?"

"Plants love water and are often thirsty," says Anna Zinnia. "Some plants love water so much they live in it. They grow just a little each day, like you who are a flower among flowers, a wonder among wonders."

I stretch my petal arms in the scented water. The second and third days pass in the sweet wetness. But no baby plant has shown even the tip of its nose.

"Did you know, my flower," asks Anna Zinnia, "that my garden is like a big library? The flowers and the bugs are like books. They have so much to tell us."

I listen as the flowers and leaves speak to me. We wait and wait some more. One day goes by, then the next. Not even the tiniest new green leaf appears in the pots.

"It's taking too long," I say to Anna Zinnia. "I want to talk to my plants."

"We can sing," says Anna Zinnia. "Plants love music. They dance and tremble under the earth, and it makes them grow faster.

"Lucy, you know the babies are beginning to sprout," she says. "The roots are pushing down, the stems are thrusting up. But the plants are hiding under the earth. Remember the secret. You must wait."

So we sing as loud as we can, louder than any bird in the garden.

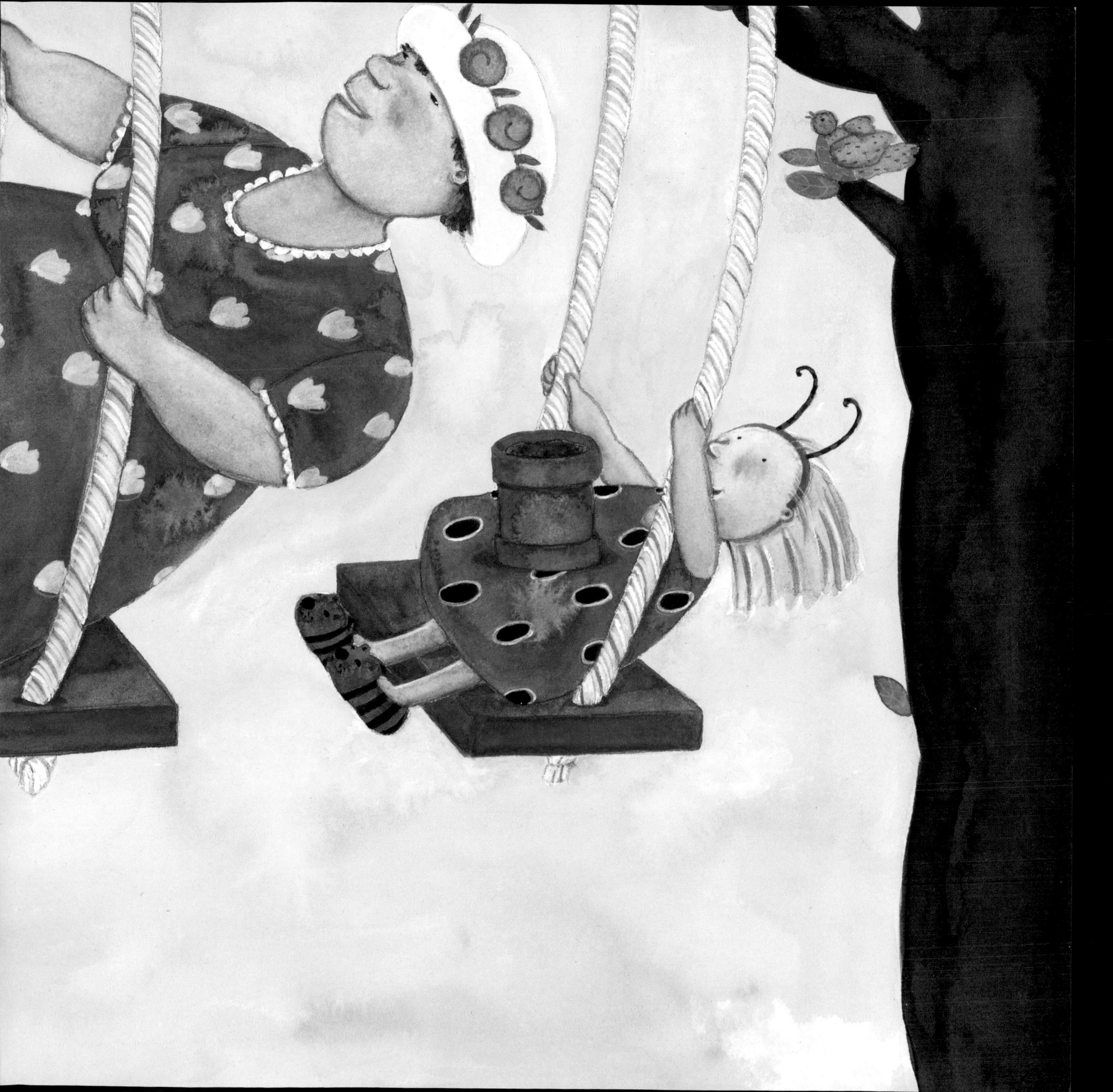

Today I can't stand it any longer. I don't want to wait anymore. We've counted the days and weeks on our fingers. I am angry. I don't want to look in the pots anymore. Why won't the baby flowers be born?

"What if the cats ate the seeds? Maybe the flowers are growing in their tummies," I say.

"Of course not," says Anna. "Let's go look. I think we might be surprised."

"How splendid," glows Anna Zinnia. "The babies have been born. Nature has given us a gift."

I bury my nose in my little sisters' petals, my beautiful little flowers. In the garden we talk for hours.

"When can we grow some more baby flowers?" I ask.